Supreme Overlord
Penelope

Grosset & Dunlap

Supreme Overlord
Penelope

By Tracey West
Illustrated by

Grosset & Dunlap

GROSSET & DUNLAP

Published by the Penguin Group
Penguin Group (USA) Inc., 375 Hudson Street, New York, New York 10014, U.S.A.
Penguin Group (Canada), 10 Alcorn Avenue, Toronto, Ontario, Canada M4V 3B2
(a division of Pearson Penguin Canada Inc.)
Penguin Books Ltd, 80 Strand, London WC2R 0RL, England
Penguin Ireland, 25 St Stephen's Green, Dublin 2, Ireland
(a division of Penguin Books Ltd)
Penguin Group (Australia), 250 Camberwell Road, Camberwell, Victoria 3124, Australia
(a division of Pearson Australia Group Pty Ltd)
Penguin Books India Pvt Ltd, 11 Community Centre, Panchsheel Park, New Delhi - 110 017, India
Penguin Group (NZ), Cnr Airborne and Rosedale Roads, Albany, Auckland 1310, New Zealand
(a division of Pearson New Zealand Ltd)
Penguin Books (South Africa) (Pty) Ltd, 24 Sturdee Avenue, Rosebank,
Johannesburg 2196, South Africa

Penguin Books Ltd, Registered Offices:

80 Strand, London WC2R 0RL, England

Library of Congress Cataloging-in-Publication Data

West, Tracey, 1965-
  Supreme Overlord Penelope / by Tracey West ; illustrated by Atomic Cartoons.
    p. cm. – (Atomic Betty chapter book ; #1)
  Summary: When a mission takes Betty and her snobby classmate Penelope to a planet where Penelope
is greeted as a long-awaited supreme being, Penelope's tendency to be bossy gets out of control
  ISBN 0-448-43090-9 (pbk)
  [1. Bossiness–Fiction. 2. Outer space–Fiction. 3. Interplanetary voyages–Fiction. 4. Science fiction.] I.
Atomic Cartoons. II. Title. III. Series.
  PZ7.W51937Sup 2005
  [Fic]–dc22

                                                                                    2005009342

ISBN 0-448-43890-9   10 9 8 7 6 5 4 3 2 1

CHAPTER 1

Exit, Stage Left!

*"I hang out in the woods
With seven little gnomes.
We dance the funky chicken
Whenever they come home."*

Betty cringed at the sound of Penelope singing in the hallway. It was hard not to laugh as Penelope flailed her arms in the air and nodded her head to the music.

"Sounds like the death wail of a Helios Monster from the Garga Galaxy," Betty muttered.

Penelope frowned and turned to Betty, her dark eyes flashing.

"Did you say something, Betty?" she asked.

"Uh, I said that you sounded very . . . interesting," Betty lied.

"Don't be jealous, Betty," Penelope said smugly.

"I'm a sure thing to get the lead in the school musical—but there are lots of different parts! I could really see you as a dancing gnome. That is, if you can dance."

Betty's green eyes narrowed. "Is that what you were doing before, dancing? I thought you were being attacked by bees."

Before Penelope could come up with an insult, Betty turned and walked over to her best friend, Noah.

"Hey, Betty," Noah said. "I hope you're trying out for the lead. You'd make a great Snow White—much better than Penelope."

"Thanks, Noah," Betty said. "We'll just have to see what happens."

I hope my voice doesn't sound this nervous when I audition, Betty thought. Every year the students of Moose Jaw Heights Junior High put on a play. This year it was a musical, *Don't Eat the Apple!*, based on the story of Snow White.

Betty really wanted to be in the play—but she'd barely had time to practice her audition song. *I wish that army of monkey-bots hadn't tried to invade the planet Chiquita Minoris last night,* she thought as she tried to cover a yawn. Being a secret Galactic Guardian and Defender of the Universe was always exciting. Betty wouldn't give it up for anything—but it didn't leave her with much free time.

"I'm sure I can sing better than Penelope," Betty said as Penelope's voice screeched through the hallway. "But do you really think I could get the lead?"

"Sure!" replied Noah. "You sang great at the talent show."

"Thanks!" Betty said, smiling. She took a deep breath. *Pull it together, Betty,* she told herself. *If I can battle aliens and robots almost every day, I can try out for the school play!* "Okay, I'm ready," she said. "Let's do this!"

Betty and Noah sat down in the auditorium with the rest of the students trying out for the play. One by one, their names were called.

"Penelope Lang, please report to the stage!" called Mrs. Ramirez, the drama teacher.

"I can't wait to see this," whispered Noah.

Penelope strode confidently onto the stage. Some fake trees and a row of seven garden gnome statues had been placed around to set the mood. They all had little red caps and white beards.

As the music started, Penelope began her wild funky-chicken dance.

"I hang out in the woods—whoa!"

Suddenly, Penelope tripped over a garden gnome! She fell flat on her face, knocking down the next gnome. One by one, the gnomes fell over like dominoes.

Mrs. Ramirez stood up as the entire auditorium burst into laughter.

"Are you all right, Penelope?" she asked.

But Penelope didn't answer. She ran off the stage, slamming the door behind her.

Betty couldn't help feeling bad for Penelope. "Ouch!" she exclaimed. "Poor Penelope. Maybe I should go see if she's all right."

But Mrs. Ramirez's voice rang out again.

"Betty Barrett, you're next!"

"Good luck," Noah said.

"Thanks," Betty replied, smiling.

Betty walked onto the stage, carefully stepping over the fallen gnomes. She took a deep breath. This couldn't be any harder than dodging asteroids, could it?

The music started. Betty opened her mouth. And then . . .

Beep! Beep! Beep!

The bracelet on Betty's wrist began to blink and beep. That meant only one thing: Somewhere in the galaxy, someone needed her help.

"Sorry, Mrs. Ramirez," Betty said. "Gotta go! Maybe I can take my turn a little later!"

But before Mrs. Ramirez could answer, Betty ran off the stage.

CHAPTER 2

Penelope the Party Crasher

Betty raced to the girls' bathroom. Admiral DeGill, the Commander-in-Chief of the Galactic Guardians and Defenders of the Universe, was calling her. That meant Betty had to drop *everything* and find a private place to receive her mission.

She burst through the door and closed herself in a stall. As Betty pressed a button on her bracelet, a hologram of Admiral DeGill appeared in front of her.

"Atomic Betty! This is your commander speaking!"

Despite the fact that Admiral DeGill looked exactly like an orange goldfish, he had a very commanding presence. Maybe it was his deep voice. Or his crisp blue uniform with its shiny brass buttons. Whatever it was, Betty always found herself standing at attention when the admiral called.

"Atomic Betty, reporting for duty!" Betty responded.

"Betty, we have reports that Maximus I.Q. may be planning an attack on the planet HihoHiho," Admiral DeGill said. "The Hihoians are peaceful people. Many years ago, they mined for gold and jewels underneath their planet. But the mines became unsafe, and they closed them down. Maximus wants them opened again. The entire race of Hihoians will be in danger! We need you right away!"

Betty frowned. Supreme Overlord Maximus I.Q. was Betty's worst enemy. He was always stirring up trouble somewhere in the galaxy. Stopping his latest evil plot would mean that Betty would miss her audition, but she didn't think twice about it. Saving the universe was *much* more important.

"I'm on my way! Over and out!"

Betty pressed another button on her bracelet. A small antenna rose up and began to blink. The signal would bring Betty's Hyper-Galactic Star Cruiser to her location in a matter of nanoseconds.

Before Betty could blink . . . *zap!* A flash of light surrounded her, beaming Betty up to the spaceship. Her crew, Sparky and X-5, sat at their stations.

"Hi, guys," Betty said. "Sparky, set a course for the planet HihoHiho."

But Sparky and X-5 did not move. They stared past Betty. X-5's electronic eyes blinked in surprise.

"What on earth is going on here?" a familiar voice screamed.

"Uh-oh," Betty said, her stomach sinking. She turned around to see Penelope standing there!

"I hate to break it to you—whoever you are—but we're not actually on Earth," Sparky joked.

X-5 wheeled over to Penelope. He held a

small scanner in his robot claw and waved it over Penelope's head.

"Intruder appears to be the earthling known as Penelope Lang," he said. "Please explain your presence, intruder."

Penelope took a step back. "You guys need to do the explaining!" she snapped. "I was in one of the bathroom stalls, cry—I mean, practicing my lines for the play. Then there was this weird beam of light. Then suddenly I'm here!"

Atomic Betty cringed. Penelope must have been in the girls' room, too—and been accidentally beamed into space!

Penelope scowled at them. "Something fishy is going on here. What's with the goofy costume, Betty? Is it part of your audition? It's totally weird— even for you."

In the process of transporting, Betty automatically changed into her Galactic Guardian uniform—a pink dress with white gloves, white boots, and a white helmet. It was perfect for saving the universe—but not exactly the kind of outfit you'd see in the halls of Moose Jaw Heights Junior High.

"Well, I, uh, it—" Betty began.

"And who's the ugly little boy?" Penelope asked, pointing at Sparky.

"Hey!" Sparky protested. "I'm a lieutenant in

the Galactic Guardians. And on some planets, I'm considered pretty good-looking."

"And what's with the talking tin can?" Penelope pointed at X-5.

"Incorrect. My body is composed of a titanium-steel alloy," X-5 replied.

Betty had to think fast. Her job as a Galactic Guardian was top secret. Not even her parents knew about her double life. And Penelope had the biggest mouth in the whole school. Betty had to do something or her whole secret identity would be lost!

"I demand to know what's going on!" Penelope shrieked.

"Calm down, Penelope," Betty said. "I'll explain everything in just one second."

Betty walked across the spaceship to her supply cabinet. Along the way, she stopped to whisper in Sparky's ear.

"I'll just use my mini Mind Eraser," she said. "We'll wipe out Penelope's memory of the ship. Then we'll beam her back to the girls' room, and we'll be off faster than a comet."

Sparky winked in reply.

Betty opened the metal cabinet and located the mini Mind Eraser, a tiny silver device that looked a little like a cell phone. Then she heard the ship's control panel beep. She turned back around—to find Penelope running around the ship in a frenzy!

"I've got it!" she yelled. "I'm on that TV show *Gotcha!*, right? This whole thing is some kind of practical joke. I bet there are cameras all over this place."

Penelope pressed button after button on the ship's control panel. Red lights above the buttons started flashing like crazy.

"Penelope, no!" Betty cried. She ran toward Penelope with the Mind Eraser aimed right at her. Sparky and X-5 lunged for Penelope, too.

But they were too late. The ship lurched. Then, without warning, it began to spin out of control.

Wham! Betty went flying back, crashing into the ship's wall. She landed with a thud—right on top of Sparky!

"X-5, do something!" Betty yelled.

X-5 had been tossed to the other side of the

 ship. He quickly rolled toward the control panel, then began pressing buttons. But Penelope was right by his side, pressing buttons, too.

"I'm ready for my close-up!" Penelope said.

The ship's interior lights went dark. Then a huge red light on the wall began to blink on and off. An alarm rang through the cabin.

"Jumping Jupiter!" yelled Sparky. "We're headed for a wormhole!"

"Yuck!" Penelope shrieked. "I hate worms!"

"Not worms," X-5 corrected her. "*Wormhole:* a four-dimensional tunnel in space—time being the fourth dimension—through which matter can travel."

"It's like a shortcut through space," Betty said, jumping to her feet. "X-5, what's our status? Will this wormhole speed us to our destination?"

"We are on course for HihoHiho, but the ship is traveling at maximum speed," X-5 said. "This could cause us to lose our trajectory."

"Speak English, you tongue-twisting tin can!" Sparky shouted, clutching the sides of his chair as the ship lurched again.

"We could miss the planet and go spiraling into eternity," X-5 said.

"Miss the planet and go spiraling into eternity? Is that all?" Sparky asked sarcastically.

"Activate the emergency slowdown system, now!" Betty ordered.

X-5 pulled on a lever. The ship began to slow down.

"That was close," Betty said.

But Penelope pushed X-5 aside.

"Cool special effects!" she said. "My turn to be the captain."

Penelope pressed a button on the control panel.

"No!" Betty yelled.

The ship sped up again and started shaking. Then everything went black. Time seemed to stand still for a moment. Betty felt like she couldn't move. A weird tingling sensation took over her whole body.

Then, suddenly, all lights in the ship went back on again. Daylight poured through the spaceship windows. Betty could see a small planet just below them.

X-5 was back at the control panel again.

"We have passed through the wormhole," X-5 announced. "I am trying to regain control of the ship."

Betty snapped back into action. She had to get Penelope under control. She just needed to use the Mind Eraser . . .

Betty looked down at the floor. The Mind Eraser had slipped from her hand while they were in the wormhole and had shattered into pieces. Things did not look good.

Then they got worse.

"Assume crash positions," X-5 called out.

"Crash positions? I thought you were regaining control of the ship!" Sparky yelled.

"I failed," X-5 said. "The ship is damaged."

"Are there going to be more special effects?" asked Penelope.

"Uh, yeah," Betty said. "So look out!"

Betty slammed Penelope to the floor and covered her with her body. There was a sickening thud as the spaceship crashed on the planet. The lights flashed on and off. Pieces of metal flew around the ship's cabin.

Then everything settled. Betty stood up, shaken. Penelope got to her feet, brushing dust off of her black skirt.

"What are you trying to do, kill me?" Penelope screamed. "This is the worst television show ever!"

CHAPTER 3

Ready to Pounce

Light-years away, Supreme Overlord Maximus I.Q. stood in front of his full-length mirror. He smoothed his long, red robe and flicked his tail back and forth. Maximus's yellow eyes narrowed as he looked at his reflection, and he frowned.

"There's something missing, Minimus," Maximus said. "I am Supreme Overlord of the Universe, after all. I should look the part. I need something shiny. Something sparkling. Something . . . expensive!"

Minimus, his Portable Underling, looked like a smaller, scrawnier, flea-bitten version of his master, with one exception. Minimus was engineered with a Swivel Head. One side of his head was a scared-looking face that sucked up to Maximus with every word. The other side was a scowling face that grumbled and mumbled.

Minimus swiveled his head around to show the scowling face. "Maybe you just need some dandruff shampoo," he muttered.

"*What* did you say?" Maximus asked.

"I mean, no metals are a match for you!" Minimus said as his head spun around to show the meek-looking, obedient face.

"Hmm. How are our plans for the invasion of HihoHiho?" Maximus asked. "Those tiny aliens used to make the finest jewels in the galaxy. They're just what I need to adorn my evil form."

Minimus's head still showed the meek-looking, obedient face. "The plan is underway, your most evilness," Minimus reported.

He pressed a button, and an image appeared on a computer screen. It showed a peaceful-looking village populated by short men with white beards and red caps. They whistled happy tunes as they watered flowers and gathered vegetables from their gardens.

"These are the Hihoians," Minimus said. "They closed their mines eons ago. Our robot scouts are surveying the planet now to find the locations of the mines. Once we find them, we will begin the invasion."

"Tell them to hurry up!" Maximus snapped, shouting directly into Minimus's face. "I've been invited to a cocktail party on the planet Tiki. I want to wow everyone there."

"Oh, you will, Maximus," Minimus grumbled. His head swiveled again as he walked away. "And if the jewels don't work, you'll knock them all out with your bad breath!"

CHAPTER 4

All Hail Penelope?

Back on the Hyper-Galactic Star Cruiser, Betty rushed over to her crew. "Sparky, X-5, are you all right?" she asked.

Sparky crawled out from under a fallen chair. His blue hair had turned white with dust.

"I feel like I've been rolled over by a moon rover," Sparky said. "But I'm still as good-lookin' as always."

"I am not damaged," X-5 reported. "But the Hyper-Galactic Star Cruiser is."

Betty frowned. *Commander DeGill is counting on us to stop Maximus's invasion of the planet HihoHiho. We can't let him down!* she thought. *We've got to repair the Hyper-Galactic Star Cruiser and get this mission back on track.*

"What kind of damage are we looking at?" Betty asked.

"Navigation systems, inoperable. Jet propulsion systems, inoperable. Communication systems, inoperable. Life support systems, inoperable . . ." X-5 began.

"Can you give us the short version?" Sparky asked.

"Nothing works," X-5 replied. "We can't go anywhere, call anybody, or find out where we are."

"You mean we don't know if we landed on HihoHiho?" Betty asked.

"The wormhole may have put us off course," X-5 answered. "I can't find out until I repair the ship."

"How long will that take?" Betty asked.

X-5's eyes flashed as his computer brain calculated the answer.

"Estimated time of repair, seventy-two hours, fifteen minutes, and seventeen seconds," X-5 said.

Betty went over the situation in her mind. She might have been nervous about trying out for the play, but in a space emergency, she knew exactly what to do.

First, they had to learn their location. If they weren't on HihoHiho, they'd have to get there—fast. They had to repair the ship. Then they had to stop Maximus. And *then* they had to fix the Mind Eraser and get Penelope back to Earth.

It was a big challenge—but not too big for Atomic Betty!

"Here's the plan," Betty announced. "X-5, you begin repairs on the ship. Sparky and I will explore the planet. We'll try to find out where we are and make sure the inhabitants here are friendly. For every friendly planet in the universe, there's one crawling with nasty aliens who like to eat space travelers. We'll report back in an hour."

"What about me?" Penelope asked. "Don't I get to be in this scene?"

Betty bit her lip. Until the Mind Eraser was fixed, she might as well let Penelope think she was on a TV show. It seemed to make her happy—and keep her from asking questions.

"You get to stay here with X-5," Betty said. "It's a very exciting scene. X-5 will perform some diagnostic tests on the ship's equipment—"

"That doesn't sound very exciting to me," Penelope snapped. "Besides, I'm not doing another thing without a tall skim mocha latte. Aren't there any production assistants around here?"

Penelope pushed through the spaceship door and stepped onto the strange planet. Betty and Sparky looked at each other and shook their heads.

"Guess we're stuck with her," Betty said. "Sorry, Sparky."

Sparky shrugged. "If there are any hungry aliens out there, maybe they'll eat her first," he said hopefully.

Betty and Sparky followed Penelope outside. The planet looked fairly normal. The ship had crashed in a field of yellow-green grass. In the distance grew crooked trees with pink and blue leaves.

Penelope was stomping across the field. "Where is my trailer? I need to fix my makeup. And I want that latte!"

"It's just past those trees," Betty said. "Come on, we'll go with you."

"Typical," Penelope said. "Always following in my shadow."

Maybe I should stop "following in your shadow" and leave you here forever! Betty thought angrily. But she quickly put the thought out of her mind. She was a Galactic Guardian, after all. Her sworn mission was to help life-forms all over the universe—even life-forms like Penelope.

Penelope stomped on, muttering about her trailer. Betty and Sparky whispered to make sure Penelope couldn't hear them as they checked the equipment on their utility belts.

"My laser is working," Sparky reported, testing the laser gun he carried.

"My bracelet seems to be fine," Betty said. "Let me try contacting Admiral DeGill." She pushed a button on her bracelet. "Admiral DeGill, Atomic Betty reporting. Over."

But there was no reply.

Betty frowned. "Maybe it's broken."

"Or maybe we're too far away for the signal to reach the admiral," Sparky pointed out. "We went through a wormhole, remember?"

"Right," Betty said. "Let's see if I can get X-5."

Betty pressed another button, and a hologram of X-5 appeared in front of her.

"We're just testing our equipment," Betty explained.

"Good idea," said X-5. "Have you discovered any life-forms yet?"

"Not yet," Betty replied. "We'll let you know when we find something."

Up ahead, Penelope stopped abruptly. "I'm tired of walking!" she whined. "I want a limo!"

"It's not much farther," Betty said. She didn't want to turn back until she found some sign of life. "Just over that hill there."

"You'd better be right," Penelope grumbled. "I thought being on TV would be a lot more glamorous."

They climbed to the top of a nearby hill and looked down.

Betty gasped. "Is that what I think it is?"

In the valley below stood a statue that was as tall as a six-story building. It was carved out of some kind of shiny white stone.

And it looked exactly like Penelope!

Hundreds of aliens circled the statue. They were small—about Sparky's height—with purple skin. They all wore green shirts and blue pants or skirts.

"Nice statue," Penelope remarked. "Is that part

of the TV show? Wait, I know—it's a marker for my dressing room, right? I *am* the star of this show, after all."

Penelope headed down the hill.

"Hey!" she yelled. "Can one of you extras get me a latte?"

The aliens looked up. Their purple eyes grew wide.

"It is our leader!" one of the aliens exclaimed.

"The prophecy has come true!" cried another.

Then they began to swarm around Penelope.

"Hail! Hail! Hail!" they chanted.

Four of the aliens picked up Penelope and carried her through the crowd. Penelope grinned.

"Now this is more like it!"

CHAPTER 5

Large and in Charge

"What are all those purple guys doing?" Sparky asked.

Betty shook her head in disbelief. "They seem to think Penelope is their leader," she replied.

"Penelope?" Sparky asked. He ran ahead. "Hey, if you guys want a leader, how about me? I'm a lot more fun than Penelope!"

The crowd of aliens ignored Sparky as they carried Penelope through a busy village. When the aliens in the village saw Penelope, they cried out in surprise and joined the crowd. They were so excited about Penelope's arrival that they didn't even notice Betty and Sparky trailing behind them.

Betty and Sparky kept to the back of the crowd, cautiously following along. The planet looked friendly, and the people there seemed happy. But a Galactic Guardian was always on guard.

The crowd grew larger and larger as they walked. Penelope smiled and waved at the aliens. Finally, they stopped in front of a large building. It had a high, wide front door and two towers on either side.

"Looks like some kind of a palace," Sparky remarked.

"Take her to the manager!" one of the aliens yelled.

The crowd parted, and the aliens carrying Penelope marched through the door.

"Let's go!" Betty told Sparky.

They rushed forward and followed the aliens inside the palace. The door opened to a large room filled with file cabinets. An alien wearing a cream

shirt, blue tie, and blue pants sat behind the desk. He had purple skin like all of the others. When he saw Penelope, his eyes widened.

"The prophecy has come true!" he cried. He ran out from behind his desk and bowed in front of Penelope. "Hail, Beloved Ruler!"

"Let me down!" Penelope snapped to the aliens carrying her. They immediately obeyed.

Then the alien in the tie noticed Betty and Sparky. "Who are these two?" he asked. "They are not in the prophecy."

Penelope smoothed out her skirt. "Don't worry about them; they're nobodies. I'm the star. And I'm thirsty. I need a latte!"

The alien motioned to one of the others.

"Would a glass of snorg juice do?" he asked. "It's very tasty."

Penelope rolled her eyes. "Figures you can't get a latte around here. This must be a real low-budget show."

Betty decided it was time to take charge. She stepped in front of the alien.

"I'm Atomic Betty, Galactic Guardian," she told him. "I think there's a little mix-up here. You see, my friend Penelope accidentally got beamed aboard our spaceship. Then we crashed on your planet. Penelope is not your long-lost leader."

But the little alien smiled. "Ah, but it's just as the prophecy said it would be!" he replied. "My name is Pendleton, and this is the planet Penelepus X. Eons ago, the ancient prophets of Penelepus X said that a powerful leader would descend from the sky. They even knew what she would look like."

Pendleton walked to one of the file cabinets. He began to flip through the files.

"Let's see, it should be under 'B' for Beloved Ruler," he muttered. "Here it is!"

Pendleton opened the file. An old scroll had the prophecy written on it in strange markings. There was also a drawing—and it looked just like Penelope!

One of the aliens handed Penelope a glass of green juice.

"What's this? Some kind of health smoothie?" Penelope asked. She took a sip, then spit it out. "This is terrible!" she screamed.

The little alien bowed nervously. "So sorry, Beloved Ruler. Can I get you something else?

Anything? Your wish is my command."

Penelope started to bark another order, then stopped.

"Wait a second," she said. "Am I really the leader? Of the whole entire planet?"

"Yes, Beloved Ruler," Pendleton said.

"That means you have to do whatever I say?" Penelope asked.

"Yes, Beloved Ruler."

Uh-oh, Betty thought. *Plain old Penelope is bad enough. But Penelope with unlimited power? That's something I never want to see!*

Penelope's dark eyes gleamed. "This is the part I was born to play!" she said. "Now let me see . . . you'll do anything I want . . ."

Penelope dumped the glass of snorg juice on the floor.

"You!" she shouted, pointing to one of the aliens. "Clean up that mess. Then get me a real latte, now!"

"Yes, Beloved Ruler," the alien said, bowing. Then he quickly left the room.

Penelope turned to the other aliens.

"You! Get me a mirror so I can check my makeup," she said, pointing to one. "The lighting in here is terrible."

"Yes, Beloved Ruler."

Penelope pointed to another alien. "And I want you to fan me. It's hot in here, and I don't like to sweat."

"Yes, Beloved Ruler," said the alien. He quickly ran off.

Penelope pointed to the fourth alien. "Find me the latest issue of *Celebrity* magazine. I want to see what everyone's wearing this spring."

"Yes, Beloved Ruler."

Penelope walked behind Pendleton's desk and sat down in his chair.

"I think I'll take this," she said. "Every leader needs a command center, right?"

"Yes, Beloved Ruler," Pendleton said, bowing.

Betty couldn't take it anymore.

"Are you really going to let her treat you like that?" she asked.

"We are happy to serve our Beloved Ruler," Pendleton said.

"That's another thing," Penelope interrupted. "This Beloved Ruler thing is getting on my nerves. You should call me something else. Something more . . . powerful."

Penelope looked thoughtful. Then a wide grin spread across her face.

"I've got it!" she cried. "How about Supreme Overlord Penelope? I like the sound of that."

"Remind you of anyone we know?" Betty whispered to Sparky.

Sparky gulped. "She sure does," he replied. "This can't be good!"

CHAPTER 6

HihoHiho— Oh No!

Sparky was right. The Penelepuns did everything Penelope asked—no matter how difficult or demanding she was. Within minutes, they had figured out how to make a skim mocha latte. Penelope sipped it and read a magazine as two aliens fanned her with long purple feathers.

Pendleton left the chamber and came back a few minutes later with a group of Penelepuns carrying a heavy gold throne. The arms and legs were encrusted with sparkling jewels.

"This golden throne was made centuries ago in anticipation of your arrival, Supreme Overlord Penelope," said Pendleton. "Please, you must sit in it. A simple chair is not good enough for our Beloved Ruler."

"I said quit it with the Beloved Ruler rap," Penelope snapped. She stood up, and the Penelepuns whisked the chair out from under her and put the throne in its place. Penelope sat back down.

"You're right, Pendleton," Penelope said. "This is a much better seat for someone as important as I am."

"I hate to say it, but Penelope makes a pretty good supreme overlord," Sparky joked.

"There is nothing good about being a supreme overlord," Betty replied. *Maximus is probably attacking HihoHiho right now—and I'm powerless to stop him!* Betty thought. *I've got to find a way off of this planet—fast.*

"I can't take this anymore," she told Sparky. "I'm going to see if X-5 needs any help."

"I'll come with you," Sparky replied.

"I need you to keep an eye on Penelope,"

Betty said. "Maybe get to know the Penelepuns. When the ship is fixed, we've got to take Penelope with us. I just hope the Penelepuns don't put up a fight. If the whole planet is against us . . ."

Sparky cast a worried look at the purple aliens.

"They might give us a hard time," he said. "They seem to really love Penelope. I just don't get it."

"Me neither," Betty agreed. "This is even stranger than the time we went to planet Sdrawkcab, and everyone ate dessert for breakfast!"

Betty left the palace and made her way back through the village. The Penelepuns had looked happy when she first saw them. Now they looked anxious and frenzied. Many were loading up wheelbarrows with what looked like blocks of white cheese. Betty stopped one of the Penelepun men. Like the rest of the Penelepun men, he wore a green shirt and blue pants.

"What's going on?" Betty asked.

"Supreme Overlord Penelope desires something called the world's largest pizza," the alien explained. "We are all giving up our cheese supplies to please her."

Betty frowned. "You're giving up all of your cheese?"

The man looked down at his shoes.

"Nothing is too good for our Beloved Ruler," he said quickly, but Betty could tell he didn't really mean it.

Maybe all of the Penelepuns aren't so happy about their new ruler, Betty thought as she watched the alien hurry off.

Betty reached the giant statue of Penelope and shuddered. It really did look just like her. What if

there was something to that Penelepun prophecy after all? It was too weird.

She climbed up the hill, then made her way through the trees until she came to the crash site. X-5 was busily repairing a strip of metal on the outside of the ship.

"How's it going, X-5?" Betty asked.

"I am making satisfactory progress," X-5 reported. "Repairs should be complete in sixty-nine hours."

Betty thought of all the trouble Penelope could cause in sixty-nine hours—not to mention what Maximus could do if she didn't stop him—and she shuddered again.

"Here's the thing, X-5," Betty said. "We have a problem."

Betty told X-5 all about how the Penelepuns thought Penelope was their destined ruler and how

Penelope was bossing them around.

"Ah, Penelepus X," X-5 said. "A planet known for its peaceful ways and colorful vegetation. I should have computed that we had crashed here."

"It might be peaceful now, but it won't be for long," Betty said. "Not with Penelope running things. Is there any way we can get out of here faster?"

"Negative," X-5 said. "Not without the use of a certified spaceship repair technician."

Betty frowned. "Penelepus X looks like a pretty primitive planet. But I'll see what I can find out," she said.

"Excellent," said X-5. "I will keep working."

"Thanks, X-5," Betty replied.

Betty rushed back to the palace. Pendleton seemed smart. He could tell her if there were any scientists around that could help X-5.

She found Pendleton kneeling before Penelope's throne.

"Your world's largest . . . er . . . pizza is ready, Supreme Overlord," he said.

"Finally!" Penelope cried. "That took long enough."

Pendleton led Penelope out of the chamber to a huge, round courtyard. Along the way, Penelepuns flung purple flower petals at Penelope's feet as she walked. The entire surface of the courtyard was covered with a giant cheese pizza. Betty had never seen anything like it.

"Your pizza, Supreme Overlord," Pendleton said. "Are you pleased?"

Penelope looked shocked. But it wasn't a happy kind of shocked.

"I SAID PEPPERONI!" Penelope screamed. "Can't you purple freaks do anything right?"

"I am so sorry, Supreme Overlord," said Pendleton. "But we do not know what pepperoni is."

Penelope turned and stormed back to her throne. The Penelepuns frantically tossed flower petals at her feet as she stomped.

Sparky spotted Betty. "Think that was bad? You should have seen her when she found out her latte was made from catterworm milk," he said.

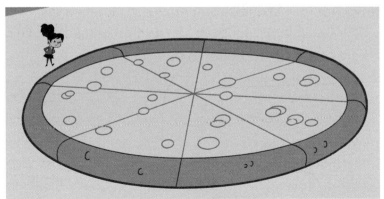

"She's terrible," Betty said. "X-5 needs help to get the repairs done faster. Have you noticed any spaceships on this planet? We need another repair technician."

Sparky shook his head. "Nope," he said. "I've been too busy stirring tomato sauce."

"Let's talk to Pendleton," Betty suggested.

But the manager of Penelepus X was busy being yelled at by Penelope.

"What a disaster!" she shrieked. "Your Supreme Overlord is not happy."

"So sorry, Supreme Overlord," Pendleton said nervously.

"You need to make me happy," Penelope said. "I think some nice jewels would do it. Maybe some gold and diamonds and emeralds. I need some bling bling fit for a ruler."

Pendleton bowed nervously. "I am afraid we have nothing like that on Penelepus X," he said.

"What do you mean?" Penelope asked. "This throne is loaded with gold and jewels."

"I can explain," Pendleton said.

Pendleton pushed a button on his desk. A holographic image showing a circle of planets appeared, hovering over the desktop.

"This is Penelepus X," he said, pointing to one of the planets. Then he gestured to a small green planet nearby. "And this is our neighbor, the planet HihoHiho."

I can't believe it, Betty thought. *We've been right next to HihoHiho the whole time!*

"HihoHiho is home to rich underground mines of gold and jewels," Pendleton continued. "That is where our ancestors got the materials for the throne. But the mines began to collapse, putting the lives of the miners in danger. So they stopped mining. No jewels have come from the planet for hundreds of years."

Penelope got a dangerous look in her eyes. "But the jewels are still there, right?" she asked.

"Yes, Supreme Overlord," Pendleton answered.

"Then it's simple!" cried Penelope. "We will invade HihoHiho and enslave the inhabitants. Then they will have to mine jewels for us."

"Penelope, that's just rotten!" Betty said.

"Besides, how are you going to invade HihoHiho without any spaceships?" Sparky asked.

"Well, actually . . ." Pendleton said.

"You've got spaceships?" Penelope asked. "Show them to me!"

Pendleton led them through the palace to the very top floor. He pressed the button and bright white light flooded the room.

Small purple spaceships shaped like pods filled the room. There must have been two hundred, Betty guessed.

"Nice going, Sparky," Betty whispered.

Sparky shrugged. "How was I supposed to know?"

"Our scientists created these so that we could search the universe for our Beloved Ruler," Pendleton explained. "But now, of course, she has come to us."

Penelope's face glowed with excitement.

"Let the invasion begin!" she yelled.

CHAPTER 7

X-5 Meets P-6

"Now she *really* reminds me of Maximus," Betty whispered to Sparky.

"Why is it that supreme overlords just want to invade planets all the time?" Sparky asked. "Don't they have any other hobbies?"

Pendleton looked very upset. "But Supreme Overlord, the Hihoians are our friends!"

"If they were our friends, they would give us their jewels," Penelope said. "Now start the invasion!"

Pendleton bowed his head. "It will take some time," he said. "The ships need to be refueled, and the pilots need training . . ."

"Well, get going, then!" Penelope snapped. "I'll be working on a design for my crown."

Penelope turned and left the room.

"Pendleton, you can't do this," Betty said urgently. "You don't have to do everything Penelope says!"

"But she is our Beloved Ruler . . ." Pendleton's voice trailed off. He didn't sound like he meant it anymore. "Ancient laws say we must obey."

Betty sighed. "I bet your prophecy doesn't say if she would be a good leader, does it?"

Pendleton looked thoughtful. "No, it doesn't."

"And it doesn't say that Penelope has to be your leader forever," Betty said. "If you don't like her, who says you have to let her stick around?"

Pendleton bit his lip. "I hate to say it, but she *has* been rather difficult," he said. "Not at all what we expected."

"Then Sparky and I can help you," Betty said. "We will get Penelope out of here. But first we need help to fix our ship."

Pendleton nodded. "Of course," he said. "I have just the thing."

Pendleton led them to a metal cabinet at the end of the room. He opened it up to reveal a robot.

"This is the robot P-6," Pendleton explained. "He's specially trained in ship building and repair. He's been in sleep mode for a few years now."

"Can we borrow him?" Betty asked eagerly.

"I don't see why not," Pendleton said. "So if he helps fix your ship, then you can leave Penelepus X?"

Betty nodded. "Yes. And we'll get your Beloved Ruler—I mean Penelope—out of here."

"All right," Pendleton said. "But as long as Supreme Overlord Penelope remains here, we must obey her. We must prepare for the invasion."

"I understand," Betty said. *I just hope that X-5 can fix the ship in time, now that he has help.*

Pendleton raced out, looking nervous.

"Sparky, do what you can to stop the invasion," Betty said. "I'm taking P-6 to the ship."

"Sure, give me the easy job," Sparky complained.

"If anyone can do it, you can, Sparky," Betty replied. "Now let's get this P-6 started."

Betty found a button on the back of P-6 and pressed it. The robot's eyes lit up a bright shade of green.

"Robot P-6, entering awake mode."

"P-6, we need your help," Betty said. "Follow me."

P-6 followed Betty through the village, back to the crashed ship. They found X-5 inside the Hyper-Galactic Star Cruiser, reprogramming the control panel. He stopped when Betty and P-6 entered.

"X-5, I'd like you to meet P-6," Betty said. "He's well trained in ship repair and maintenance. Maybe one of you can work on the ship, and the other one can fix the mini Mind Eraser."

X-5 rolled up to P-6. "You look familiar," he said.

"Impossible," said P-6. "I have never left the coordinates of Penelepus X."

"Correct," said X-5. "But I may have seen your image in my database."

"Once again, impossible," said P-6. "My image has never been catalogued."

"I disagree," said X-5. "There is an 87 percent probability that—"

"Enough, you guys," Betty said. "Let's get to work. We've got to get this ship off the ground!"

CHAPTER 8

Sparky to the Rescue!

Back at the palace, Sparky tried his best to get through to the Penelepuns. He found the pilots gathered outside by the fleet of ships.

"Hear me, Penelepuns!" Sparky called to the pilots. He stood up on a spaceship. "Penelope is a horrible leader! You—"

"Be quiet!" exclaimed one of the pilots, looking around nervously. "What if she hears you?"

Sparky rolled his eyes. "No way. She's busy designing a jeweled pair of shoes to wear with her jeweled crown. She won't come out of the palace for hours!" Sparky cleared his throat. "Where was I? Oh, yeah—you don't have to do this!"

"Um, yes we do," replied one of the pilots. "Penelope is our Supreme Overlord."

"Maybe you're wrong," Sparky said. "Maybe she's not the right one."

"But she looks just like the statue!" someone called out.

"That's true," Sparky admitted.

"And she fell from the sky!" someone else yelled.

"Yeah, you're right," Sparky said. "All right. Let's say she is your Supreme Overlord. Who says you have to obey her?"

"She does!" the pilots cried.

Sparky tapped his chin. "You've got a point there," he said. "Okay, okay. So you have to obey her. But maybe you can do it . . . badly."

The Penelepun pilots looked thoughtful. They began to whisper among themselves. Then someone called out, "What exactly do you mean?"

"Well, you have to obey Penelope by invading HihoHiho," Sparky said. "But maybe you can just not do a very good job of it. Then you'd still be obeying her. Get it?"

The Penelepuns looked confused. Then one of them looked hopeful. He raised his hand.

"You mean we could, perhaps, fly very slowly?"

"Exactly!" Sparky said.

"And when we enslave the Hihoians, we could do it . . . nicely?" the pilot asked.

"Why not?" Sparky said. "Who said invaders can't be polite?"

A murmur went through the chamber.

"Okay!" said the pilots. "We'll do it your way!"

"Hooray!" Sparky cheered. Sure, it wasn't exactly what Betty wanted.

But it was the best he could do for now.

CHAPTER 9

Robot Face Off!

Betty and the robots were hard at work repairing the spaceship—but things weren't going as smoothly as Betty had hoped.

"Betty, P-6 is charging the centrifixial cable before charging the exterior drive," X-5 said.

"Of course," said P-6. "That is the most efficient way to do it."

"I disagree," said X-5. "That method is only 98.9 percent efficient."

"Stop arguing, you two!" Betty cried. "We've got to save the Hihoians!"

The robots went back to work.

"My method is the most efficient," P-6 grumbled.

"Is not," said X-5.

"Is too!" said P-6.

Betty sighed and wiped the rocket refueling grease off her hands. The robots just could not get along! She was about to raise her voice again when X-5 turned to her.

"Seventy percent of the systems are currently online," X-5 announced. "We just need to finish repair of the fuel core."

"Excellent!" Betty cried. She turned on the large viewer screen. "Let's see what's happening on HihoHiho."

Betty programmed the viewer. An image of a village appeared on the screen. The tiny inhabitants looked just like garden gnomes, with white beards, green shirts, and tan pants. They moved around happily, whistling as they tended to their gardens.

"Good," Betty said. "The invasion hasn't started."

Suddenly, a cry went up from the Hihoians on screen. Hundreds of pod-shaped ships hovered in the sky above them.

"The Penelepun fleet has arrived," P-6 announced.

"I was just going to say that," said X-5.

"That's weird," Betty said. "They seem to be flying really slowly."

"That is not all that is weird," said X-5. "Look."

X-5 pressed buttons on the control panel, zooming in on a portion of the screen. Hovering below the Penelepun fleet was a steel gray robot with a red glowing eye.

"That's one of Maximus's robots!" Betty cried.

She turned to X-5 and P-6.

"Get this ship ready, boys!" she said urgently. "We've got two invasions to stop now!"

CHAPTER 10

Cranky Kitty

Supreme Overlord Maximus I.Q. tapped his sharp claws against the desktop. "I am very anxious for word from HihoHiho, Minimus," he said. "Where is that scouting robot's report?"

"It should be here any moment, your eminence," Minimus replied.

At that moment, the control monitor lit up with an image of the robot.

Minimus's head swirled around. "It's about time," he complained.

"Present your report immediately," Maximus demanded. "Those glittering jewels are just waiting to be plucked for my pleasure."

"Location of mines has been determined," the

robot said in a mechanical voice. "But there is one difficulty."

More images flashed across the monitor. Maximus's eyes narrowed as he saw the pod ships flying over HihoHiho.

"What's this? Someone else is invading my planet? Who is behind all of this?"

The image on the screen changed. This time, it showed a close-up of Penelope. She was riding in one of the pods, seated behind a Penelepun pilot.

"I want those mines opened up right now!" Penelope yelled into her communicator. "Supreme Overlord Penelope needs a crown!"

Maximus stood up. "This is an outrage!" he shouted.

Minimus's head swiveled back around. "Yes, an outrage," he replied meekly.

Maximus began to pace around the room.

"She dares to call herself Supreme Overlord? Who does she think she is? I am the only Supreme Overlord in the galaxy!"

Minimus's head swiveled once again. "Well, there is Supreme Overlord Gary in the Alpha Quadrant. And don't forget—"

"Silence!" Maximus fumed. "We must put a stop to this—immediately! Begin the invasion of HihoHiho!"

Minimus's head swerved back again. "Oh, Master, the planet is already being invaded," he whined.

"Then we will invade the invasion!" Maximus cried. "Nobody steals my jewels. Even if they don't belong to me in the first place!"

Minimus bowed. "Very well, Your Magnificence," he said. Then he scurried out.

Maximus moved his face close to the computer screen.

"Have your fun now, Penelope," he growled. "When I get through with you, you will regret the day you ever came across Supreme Overlord Maximus I.Q.!"

CHAPTER 11

The Polite Invasion

"Estimated time of repair, thirty minutes," X-5 gave Betty an update.

"That's too long!" Betty said. "Are the transporters working?"

"Affirmative," said P-6.

"Beam me to the palace, now!" Betty ordered. "Then meet me on HihoHiho as soon as you can."

Seconds later, Betty materialized in the ship docking station of the palace. Sparky was addressing the last of the Penelepun army before they took off.

"Don't forget—fly slowly! And you don't have to hurt the Hihoians!" he said. Then he saw Betty. "Sorry, Chief. I did my best! But I couldn't stop them from obeying their 'Beloved Ruler.'"

Betty jumped into an empty space pod. "Get back to the ship. I'm going to stop the invasion. I'll meet you there."

"Roger, Captain!" Sparky said.

Betty quickly examined the controls of the space pod, then activated the thrusters and flew out of the palace. As she zoomed toward HihoHiho, her pod almost grazed the head of the giant Penelope statue. *I knew a giant Penelope would be trouble,* Betty thought with a scowl. *Wait a minute . . . that gives me an idea . . .*

"Hey, Sparky," she said over the communicator. "I need you to bring something with you when you come to HihoHiho. I've got a plan. A really BIG plan . . ."

Down on HihoHiho, the invading Penelepuns stormed a village and surrounded the Hihoians. The white-bearded aliens were about the same size as the Penelepuns. They eyed the invaders suspiciously. And they all held sharp-looking garden tools.

One of the Penelepuns stepped forward.

"We come in the name of Supreme Overlord Penelope!" said the Penelepun. "We demand that you open your mines and dig up your jewels!"

One of the pilots nudged the Penelepun and whispered in his ear.

"Sorry," the Penelepun corrected himself. "I meant to say, would you mind going into your mines and getting some jewels for us? Please?"

"Um, let me think about it," said a Hihoian. "No way!"

The Hihoians began to wave their garden tools. The Penelepuns stepped back, afraid.

Suddenly, a space pod swooped down from the sky.

"Attention, people of HihoHiho!" Penelope screeched through a microphone. "I am Supreme Overlord Penelope. I demand that you open your mines and dig up some gold and jewels right now!"

"Let's see you make us!" said one white-bearded alien.

Penelope grinned. "If you insist!"

A laser beam shot into the crowd of Hihoians, and they scattered. Some dropped their garden tools. The Penelepuns picked them up.

"You heard her," said one Penelepun. "Now get moving! Uh, please!"

The Hihoians warily looked at Penelope's ship. Then the little gnomelike people all moved to a boarded-up cave entrance on the hillside. While the Penelepuns prodded them, they removed the boards. Then they lined up in single file and began to march into the cave, singing a sad song.

"Hiho, hiho, we just don't want to go!"

"Don't worry! You don't have to go anywhere!"

The Hihoians looked up. Betty flew down in her space pod, coming between them and Penelope.

"Show's over, Penelope!" Betty yelled over her microphone. "Leave this planet alone. We're going home."

"Not without my jewels!" Penelope yelled back.

Zap! Zap! Zap! Penelope aimed three powerful laser blasts at Betty's pod.

Betty clutched the steering toggle and quickly careened to the left, dodging the blasts. Then she swung the pod around.

She could easily blast Penelope's ship with one shot. But unlike Penelope, Betty knew the lasers were real. She had to keep Penelope safe.

"Land your pod right now, Penelope," Betty called out.

Zap! Zap! Zap!

"Get out of here, Betty!" Penelope cried, shooting at the pod again. "You're ruining my big scene!"

Betty's stomach lurched as she steered the ship in an upside-down loop, avoiding the blasts once again. She had to think of something . . .

"But we've got to go," Betty said. "We've got to shoot a commercial!"

Penelope stopped the pod in midair. "A commercial? Really? Can I get my hair done first?"

Betty sighed with relief. "Sure," she said. "Just land the ship."

Penelope nodded to the pilot of her pod, and the ship began to descend.

Then, suddenly, a giant metal claw fell from the sky. It grabbed Penelope's pod. The jolt sent the Penelepun pilot flying out the window.

A familiar voice rang through the village.

"Now that the amateurs have finished their silly games, if anybody is going to invade this planet, it will be me—Supreme Overlord Maximus I.Q.!"

Supreme Overlord vs. Supreme Overlord

"Maximus!" Betty cried. "Let go of her, now!"

"I'm afraid I can't do that, Betty dear," Maximus snarled. "I need to have a word with this imposter. I am the only Supreme Overlord in this galaxy!"

Maximus maneuvered the crane so that Penelope's pod dangled in front of the window of his long, gray spaceship. Penelope glared at him.

"Who do you think you are?" she asked. "I am the star of this TV show!"

"I am Supreme Overlord Maximus I.Q.," Maximus replied.

"The greatest evil ruler in the universe," Minimus added.

"This totally stinks!" Penelope fumed. "No way am I going to be replaced by a guy in a cat suit! I want to talk to the director!"

Maximus grinned. "I think I will have her stuffed

and put on display at my headquarters. It will send a message to anyone else who thinks they can challenge my position as Supreme Overlord. What do you think, Minimus?"

"An excellent idea as always, your evilness," Minimus agreed.

A hatch opened up on top of the spaceship. The claw moved, ready to drop Penelope's pod in the hatch.

Betty moved quickly. She zoomed toward Maximus's ship and zapped the metal claw with her lasers. The claw swung out, sending the pod flying. Penelope tumbled out of the pod and hurled toward the surface of the planet.

"Ahhhhhhhhhhhhhhh!" Penelope screamed.

Betty quickly maneuvered her ship beneath Penelope. She pressed a button on the control panel, and a large net extended from the side door. The net scooped up Penelope, and Betty landed the pod safely on the planet's surface.

Penelope jumped out of the net. "This is ridiculous! Shouldn't a stunt woman be doing these action scenes for me? Look—I broke a nail! I need a manicure *immediately*!"

Maximus landed his ship. He stormed out, his eyes blazing.

"I am sick and tired of your meddling, Atomic Betty!" he cried. "Robot army, attack!"

CHAPTER 13

Operation Penelope Plug

A door slid open on the spaceship, and Maximus's robot army marched out. The robots had thick, square bodies, strong metal legs, and heads that looked like upside-down buckets. Each robot had a large red eye in the middle of its head.

Betty knew two things about Maximus's robots: They were fast—and they could fight. She struck a martial arts pose.

"It's time to kick some robot butt!"

Three robots charged Betty at once.

"Hee-ya!" Betty delivered a powerful kick to the first one. It flew back, knocking down the other two like dominoes.

"Betty, behind you!" one of the Hihoians cried.

Betty turned to see two more robots racing toward her.

Wham! Wham!

She dealt a swift karate chop to each one's head. The two staggered for a moment, then crashed to the ground.

From the corner of her eye, Betty saw a flash of red coming toward her. She somersaulted out of the way just as a hot laser blast from one of the robots sped past her.

Betty jumped to her feet. The robots had formed a circle around her now. She pressed a button on her bracelet. Then she stood on her toes and spun around in a circle.

Zap! Zap! Zap! Zap! Zap!

She zapped each robot with a laser beam as she spun around. They fell backward, one by one.

"Gotta thank Mom for those ballet lessons," Betty said with a laugh.

"This isn't over, Betty!" Maximus growled. More robots charged out of his ship.

Betty jumped over the fallen robots. The attacking robots had her with her back against the open mine. She looked up at the sky. Where was Sparky?

Right on cue, the Hyper-Galactic Star

Cruiser appeared overhead. Betty pressed a button on her bracelet.

"Beam me up, Sparky!" Betty cried.

Betty vanished just as the robots launched a laser attack in her direction. They converged at the mine entrance, confused.

"Perfect timing, guys!" Betty said.

"Of course," said X-5 and P-6 at the same time.

Betty jumped into her captain's chair.

"All right, Sparky," she said. "Let's deliver our payload: Operation Penelope Plug!"

The ship released its tractor beam—which had been towing the giant statue of Penelope! It crashed inside the mine entrance, crushing the robots beneath it. The huge statue completely blocked the entrance to the mine.

Sparky landed the Hyper-Galactic Star Cruiser, and Betty and her crew stepped out. The Hihoians and the Penelepuns crowded around the ship.

"Hooray!" the Hihoians cheered.

The Penelepuns looked relieved. One of them asked, "Does this mean we don't have to be invaders anymore?"

A shrieking voice answered them.

"What is going on here?" Penelope yelled. She stormed over to Atomic Betty.

Betty grinned. "Sorry. The mines are closed."

Penelope's face turned bright red. "It's not fair! I didn't get my jewels! And everybody should be cheering *me*, not you! I'm going to complain to the director!"

Penelope stormed toward Maximus's ship. "This is all your fault, you flea bag! Everything was going great until you came along!"

"How dare you!" Maximus cried. He began pressing buttons on his control panel. "Robots, attack!"

"We are all out of robots, your excellence," Minimus informed him.

Penelope pushed Maximus out of the way. "Give me that! I need to talk to the director!"

Penelope started pressing buttons on Maximus's control panel.

"Excuse me, director? I need to talk to you!" Penelope yelled.

"Foolish girl! Stop right now!" Maximus ordered.

The ship began to shake. Lights blinked on and off. A siren rang through the cabin.

"Your Eminence, we're going to take off!" Minimus cried.

"I'll just take Penelope, if you don't mind," Atomic Betty said, swooping in. She grabbed Penelope and beamed them both back to HihoHiho.

Betty was just in time. The ship lifted off and began to spiral away into the sky.

"Atomic Betty, I will get you for this!" Maximus cried.

Good-bye, Sweet Penelepuns

Betty put Penelope safely on the ground. There were bits and pieces of Maximus's robot army everywhere she looked.

"Sorry about the mess," she said to one of the Hihoians.

"That's okay," he replied. "We can use the scrap metal to make our garden tools."

The Penelepuns all got back in their space pods and returned to Penelepus X.

"Come on, Penelope," Betty said. "The director's waiting to talk to you. We'll take you to him."

"It's about time!" Penelope said. She followed Betty back onto the Hyper-Galactic Star Cruiser.

"We need to make one stop first," Betty added.

Minutes later, the ship landed outside the palace. Pendleton rushed down the stairs, a worried look on his face.

"Supreme Overlord, are you all right?" he asked.

Penelope yawned. "This is getting boring. I want to go home and be pampered properly."

Pendleton looked sad. "But you can't leave us! We've been waiting for so long!"

"Yeah, yeah, whatever," Penelope said. "I'll be in my trailer." She walked back onto the Hyper-Galactic Star Cruiser.

"Cheer up, Pendleton," Atomic Betty said. "You didn't really like having Penelope as your ruler, did you?"

Pendleton looked embarrassed. "Well . . ."

"You're a great manager," Betty said. "I'm sure the Penelepuns will be happy to have you back in charge."

In response, the Penelepuns let out a cheer.

Pendleton smiled. "Thank you, Atomic Betty. We won't forget you."

P-6 rolled away from the ship.

"Good-bye, X-5," P-6 said. "This has been an interesting and informative interaction."

"Parting is such sweet sorrow," X-5 replied.

Betty, Sparky, and X-5 boarded the Hyper-

Galactic Star Cruiser—and found Penelope sitting at the control panel!

"Is there a DVD player on this thing?" she asked, pushing a button. "I'm bored!"

"Not again!" Betty cried.

X-5 quickly rolled next to Penelope and aimed a spray of pink smoke at her face. She instantly fell asleep on the control panel.

"Sleeping Spray," said X-5. "She will awaken when we reach Earth. And you need this as well."

X-5 handed Betty the mini Mind Eraser. "The mini Mind Eraser!" Betty exclaimed. "Thanks, X-5."

Betty put the device on top of Penelope's head and pressed a button. The mini Mind Eraser glowed softly.

"That does it," Betty said. "By the time we get home, Penelope won't remember a thing that's happened."

"Good!" Sparky said.

"I wish I could forget, too," Betty added. "Penelope as Supreme Overlord? I don't know who is worse—her or Maximus!"

"Or both!" X-5 said. Everyone laughed.

"Contacting Atomic Betty," Admiral DeGill's voice rang out as the commander's image appeared on their communication screen.

"HihoHiho is safe, sir," Betty said. "I will submit a full report in the morning."

"Excellent work, Atomic Betty," DeGill replied. "I knew I could count on you!"

Admiral DeGill signed off. Betty looked around the ship at Penelope's sleeping form. This mission could have been a disaster—but Betty and her crew had come through in the end.

"Come on, guys," Betty said, smiling. "Mission accomplished. Let's get back to Earth!"

CHAPTER 15

And They All Lived Happily Ever After . . .

Betty braced herself as they entered the dark, swirling wormhole. Suddenly, the Hyper-Galactic Star Cruiser was hovering above Moose Jaw Heights Junior High School.

"Thanks, guys," Betty told Sparky and X-5. "I don't know what I'd do without you two."

"The probability of your missions succeeding would decline by 22.6 percent," X-5 said.

"Well, sure," Betty said. "But I'd miss you, too."

Betty stood next to the sleeping Penelope.

"Beam us back, please," she said.

"Your wish is my command!" Sparky said. "See ya, Betty!"

Seconds later, Penelope and Betty materialized inside a stall in the girls' bathroom. Penelope woke from her sleep.

"What are you doing here?" she snapped. "Did

you come here to make fun of me for my audition? I'd like to see you do any better!"

Betty sighed. "I came to see if you were all right," she said. "Your audition wasn't so bad."

Penelope started to sob. "It was awful! I'll never get the part of Snow White!"

Betty suddenly had an idea. "Hey, maybe Snow White isn't the best part for you. Wouldn't playing the Wicked Queen be a lot more fun? You'd get to order people around, make them worship you . . ."

A smile slowly formed on Penelope's face. "The evil queen. I like it!" she said. "That's a good idea—even if it came from a lame brain like you, Betty!"

Penelope rushed out of the girls' room, slamming the door behind her.

"You're welcome," Betty said as a smile spread over her face. *At least everything is back to normal!*

She met up with Noah in the hallway a few minutes later.

"Betty! What happened?" asked Noah. "Why'd you run out of your audition?"

"Uh, nerves, I guess," Betty lied.

"That's crazy," Noah said. "You've got a great voice."

Penelope's singing rang through the hall.

"Come on," Betty said. "Let's check it out."

Betty and Noah peeked through the stage door. Penelope was on stage, singing her heart out.

"I'm the Evil Queen.

I'm bad and I'm mean.

I'm the wickedest gal that you've ever seen!"

"Hey, she's not bad," Noah admitted.

"It's the part she was born to play," Betty said.

Mrs. Ramirez stood up and began to clap. "Wonderful, Penelope! You've got the part!"

Noah and Betty walked away from the door.

"Too bad, Betty," Noah said. "While you were gone, all of the other parts were filled."

Betty thought about her adventure on Penelepus X and smiled.

"That's okay, Noah," Betty said. "I don't think I want to live in a world where Penelope is the evil queen!"